A Letter from Santa

Yukiko Tanno   Illustrated by Mako Taruishi

PUFFIN BOOKS

It was Christmas Eve, and the snow was falling.
Postman Mouse stuffed the Christmas letters
into his post-bag, and rushed outside.

'I must hurry, I must hurry. Everyone is waiting
for their post,' he panted as he ran along.

Postman Mouse had been
scampering so fast that he slipped
on the ice and fell over.

'Oh no, all the letters have fallen
out of my post-bag!' he cried.

Postman Mouse started gathering
up the letters as quickly
as he possibly could.

But when he saw the last letter he had picked up, he let out a little cry. The snow had blurred and blotted the address on the envelope.

'What shall I do? Now I can't tell who this letter is for. Oh dear! I'd better deliver the other letters first.' So Postman Mouse began plodding on his way.

'A letter for you, Miss Rabbit.'

'Mr Crow, express mail for you.'

The animals in the forest noticed how glum Postman Mouse looked. Normally he was so cheerful.

'I wonder what's making him so miserable?' they asked each other.

When Postman Mouse had finished
delivering all the letters, he came to the
edge of the forest and took out the
remaining letter from his post-bag.

'What can I do?' he said to himself.

Just then, Mr Fox appeared. 'I was worried
about you, Postman Mouse,' he said.

Mrs Owl and Little Squirrel came too.
And then came Brown Bear, Miss Rabbit
and Mr Crow. They had all been worried about
Postman Mouse and had come to see what
was wrong.

Postman Mouse showed them the letter
with the address blotted out.

'Oh dear, this *is* a problem,' said Brown Bear.

Then Miss Rabbit asked, 'Postman Mouse,
who is the letter *from*?'

'Oh, I hadn't thought of looking at that!'
cried Postman Mouse.

Postman Mouse turned the letter
over and was very surprised.
'Why, it's from Santa!'
   'Really? Let me see!' everyone
shouted, amazed.
   'I wonder who would get a letter
from Santa?' asked Little Squirrel.
   Mr Crow said, 'It could be one
of us, couldn't it,' and everyone
just stared at each other.

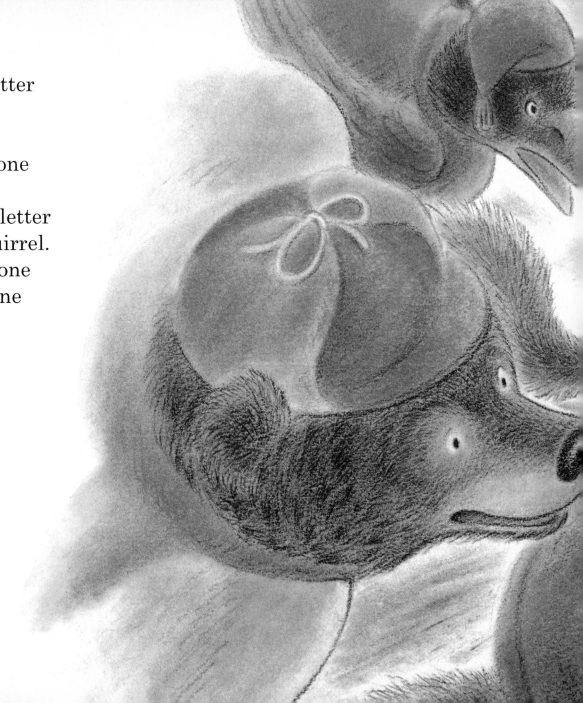

They all looked once again at the blurred address on the envelope.

'It must be for me
because of the blue
apron,' said Mrs Owl.

'Look, there's the same
black bag as mine,'
said Miss Rabbit.

'No, the letter must be
for me because there's
a hat and a woollen
scarf,' said Mr Fox.

'But aren't those *my* wellington boots? And *my* woollen scarf...?' asked Little Squirrel.

'It looks like my hat and woollen scarf too,' said Mr Crow.

'Everyone, look at my blue hat. It's a blue hat,' said Brown Bear.
'But there's something not quite right with everyone's clothes. What on earth could be? Is it a walking-stick? It could be the handle of an umbrella, or...'

'Ouch! Ouch! My tail, my tail!' squeaked a voice from behind.

Brown Bear had trodden on Postman Mouse's tail.

'I'm so sorry. Are you all right?' said Brown Bear.

And then suddenly everyone cried out, 'Oh!'

Yes, ◠ was a tail. It was Postman Mouse's tail.

'The letter is for *you*, Postman Mouse,' everyone shouted and they looked again carefully at the picture on the envelope and at Postman Mouse.

Blue hat, blue coat, red woollen
scarf, black wellington boots, and
the postman's black bag.

'There's no mistake about it.
This letter is for you, Postman
Mouse,' said Brown Bear.

'For me! A letter from Santa?'
said Postman Mouse a little shyly.

'Postman Mouse, open it and
read it!' everyone shouted happily.

Postman Mouse opened the letter and started to read it:

I am a
beginner Santa.
I would like you,
Postman Mouse
to help me deliver presents
by guiding me through
the forest. Please come to
the biggest fir tree
at dusk.
From Santa

'Santa's guide! You are so lucky,
Postman Mouse. You'll be able to ride
on Santa's sleigh,' everyone said enviously.
'Thank you, thank you everyone,' said Postman Mouse.

'You'd better hurry, Postman Mouse, it'll be dusk soon,' said Little Squirrel.

'What can I do?' asked Postman Mouse. 'The biggest fir tree is so far away that I won't get there in time.'

'Don't worry, just leave it to me,' said Brown Bear. He lifted Postman Mouse into the pocket of his overcoat and started running as fast as he could.

Mr Fox, Little Squirrel and Miss Rabbit also started to run. Mrs Owl and Mr Crow kept up with everyone by flying above their heads. The sun set and the forest became dark. Uphill and downhill, everyone ran and ran.

Suddenly they could see shining
lights in front of them. The biggest
fir tree in the forest was glowing
with hundreds and hundreds of
lights. Santa was standing in front
of the tree.

'Hello, Postman Mouse! Thank
you for coming. Let's start right
away. Do you all want a ride on the
sleigh?' Santa asked.

'Oh yes,' everyone shouted.

'Ready, Steady, Go!'

The sleigh with Postman Mouse
and everyone else on board started
to move and before they knew it,
it was gliding into the sky.

'How high it is!'

'We're flying, we're flying!'

'Look, there's your house, Mr Fox.'

'Look at all the snow falling
around us!'

Postman Mouse guided Santa so
well that Santa was able to deliver
all the presents safely.

Well done, Postman Mouse!